THE
SECRET HISTORY OF
UNICORNS

THE
SECRET HISTORY OF
UNICORNS

J. RENISON

k
Kandour Ltd

Published by

Kandour Ltd,

Monticello House,

45 Russell Square,

London,

WC1 4JP

UNITED KINGDOM

This edition printed in 2007 for Bookmart Ltd

Registered Number 2372865

Trading as Bookmart Ltd

Blaby Road, Wigston

Leicester LE18 4SE

First published 2007

10 9 8 7 6 5 4 3 2 1

Author: Jessica Renison

Editor: John Taylor

Design and Layout: Domex e-Data Pvt Ltd

Proof reader: Tobias Grimshaw

Production: Karen Lomax and Carol Titchener

Design concepts: Alex Ingr

Text and Design Copyright © Kandour Ltd 2007

Printed and bound in China

ISBN 13: 978-1-904756-97-2

Contents

he Unicorn is one of the most intriguing and magical creatures of all time. Many attempts have been made by various people of all times and from all places to capture this noble, elusive creature. Yet, its very existence remains an unsolved mystery to this day. Generally depicted as a white horse with a long, single, spiraled horn, the unicorn has stood as a symbol of love, purity, hope and majesty throughout the ages. Its silvery white coat and silver hooves make it glow like moonlight, and it is this aura of moonlight that gives the unicorn its positive spiritual energy and makes it a force for good in the world.

The unicorn, by its very nature, is a mysterious creature, not only difficult to catch but full of contradictions. For example, although a unicorn never thinks of itself first but always acts to protect others, it is nevertheless a solitary creature. It prefers most of all to be alone and to roam at peace in its own company. This sense of self-sufficiency and steady calm makes it the envy of other, more frantic beings, – particularly human beings. Evidence of this is found in a "Hymn to the Buddha", taken from the Buddhist religion, in which those who wish to find inner peace are advised, "Like the unicorn, in solitude roam". It is hardly surprising then that the solitary

A popular trick in folklore was to lull a unicorn to sleep on the lap of a virgin and then trap him in a net

unicorn, immeasurably beautiful but utterly modest, with no desire to put itself on show or attract attention, is rarely seen and often thought to be an entirely imaginary creature. But it is not! Of course! It is for real and present to those who know and love it.

Although unicorns have appeared in songs, poems and stories for centuries, it has been many years since anyone actually saw one. One possible reason for this may be that the unicorn is an auspicious creature. This means that it only appears in times when goodness reigns in the world; in dark times, it disappears. Some say that in these dark days of greed and destruction, we will never see a unicorn because it will not pollute its purity by contact with our murky world. But others say that it is only the pure in spirit who see unicorns and they can see them at any time

and in any place. Whatever the truth of the matter may be, in these pages, we will attempt to unravel some of the most secret threads in the unique and protected history of unicorns.

In the days of warts and boils on women's faces, many unicorns were said to be more beautiful than a lot of men's wives.

The unicorn is commonly associated with purity and chastity due to its blessed time in the Garden of Eden in those first days of creation.

Unicorns at the Beginning of Time

The Unicorn is said to be the first animal that Adam named when he was given the task of naming all the creatures in the **Garden of Eden**. Our name for it comes from the Latin for 'one' – unus and 'horn' – cornu, but Adam did not speak Latin as far as we know. So what he named it remains a mystery. Suffice to say that 'unicorn' is the name that has come down to us through history and certainly the

one that suits it the most. Incidentally, if you found out the words for 'one' and 'horn' in other languages, you might enjoy experimenting with different names for the unicorn. In Ancient Greek, for example, it would be called 'the Monoceros' and in German 'the Einhorn.' Because Adam had chosen to name this creature first, it was especially blessed by God. It is said that God touched the unicorn on the tip of its horn and forever after, the unicorn's horn has been a source of great strength with special healing powers.

When Adam and Eve had to leave the Garden of Eden and enter the world because of the sin they

had committed, the Unicorn was given a choice: either it could go with them into the world which was full of pain and suffering, but also full of love and joy, or it could stay in the Garden of Eden. The unicorn chose to go with Adam and Eve into the world and it remained with them as a treasured companion and a great source of consolation. The unicorn is commonly associated with purity and chastity due to

its blessed time in the Garden of Eden in those first days of creation. It is also, however, seen as a creature of great compassion and self-sacrifice, because it chose the difficult path of the world out of a sense of love and loyalty to its guardians. A medieval saint once explained that the reason a unicorn has such great strength and healing powers (which you will learn about hereafter) is that, once a year it returns to the Garden of Eden and drinks the **Water of Paradise**. Certainly, its horn having been touched by the hand of God, served it well for the world that it was to enter.

So, we know that the unicorn left the Garden of Eden and went out into the big wide world, but what happened to it after that? Well, we next hear of

it around the time of the great flood that wiped out the large majority of living beings in the world. This was some time before Christ was born. The unicorn crops up in Jewish folklore, where it is said that when **Noah** gathered two of every animal into the ark to save them from the flood, he had to leave the unicorns behind because they took up too much space with their horns. Another reason given – and this one seems somewhat suspect – is that they demanded too much attention and therefore taking them would

be too troublesome. This gives the impression that unicorns are something like spoilt princesses, who insist everyone admires their beautiful tresses all the time, and this impression does not at all match the idea of unicorns that is found elsewhere in ancient literature.

A Ukrainian folk tale has an entirely different story to tell and one far more in keeping with the unicorn's heroic spirit. It tells how the unicorns refused to enter the ark because they were confident that they would be able to swim through the flood. The flood lasted forty days and forty nights and the unicorns swam and swam, valiant and strong, but at the very last, when the rain had stopped and the

flood was nearly over, some birds who had been clinging to the side of the ark throughout the flood saw the unicorns' horns protruding out of the waves, and they went and perched on them for safety. Sadly, this was too much for the exhausted unicorns, who sank breathless, under the weight of the birds and were seen no more. So, that is how a Ukrainian folk tale tells it, but it is unlikely that unicorns were wiped out by that Biblical flood, because there have been sightings of them since those days. And who would believe that our majestic unicorns could sink under the weight of some feeble birds?

The unicorn also appears at the beginning of time in the creation stories of other traditions. According to one Eastern tradition, the universe at the point of its creation took the form of an egg. When the shell of the egg cracked, chaos spilled out in all directions. That chaos contained the five elements, the light and the dark, and the first created man. According to this tradition, four unique animals were present at the creation of the universe: the dragon, the tortoise, the phoenix, and the unicorn. After the universe had been created, a process which took eighteen thousand years – the first man died and his body became the Earth, his blood the waters, and his breath became the wind, his voice became the thunder, his eyes the sun and moon, his bones turned into stones and minerals, his hair became the vegetation, and his sweat the rain. Each of the four animals chose their own territory. The dragon

became the guardian of the waters, the tortoise went to the swamp, the phoenix flew to desert lands, and the unicorn took to the forests. Forests are the natural habitat of the unicorn, partly because they can hide behind clumps of trees and so protect themselves, and partly because forests are bursting with life and promise – thick with rich greenery and crammed with leaping, chattering animals of all sorts. This double nature of the forest means that the unicorn can maintain the privacy it so values whilst also enjoying the spark and energy of life all around him. A unicorn could never live in a dead or dry place because it is itself so full of life.

Unicorns in cave paintings

But we have started this story some time after it really started. To find out about the very beginnings of unicorns, we need to go back even further. Back and back and back into prehistory, which is a long, long time ago – before history even started.

The Secret History Of Unicorns

We are lucky enough still to have some cave paintings from prehistorical times that give us an idea of life before our own times. Studying paintings on cave walls is one way of finding out how things used to be, what creatures used to exist, what people used to do, that sort of thing.

Interestingly, there is a cave painting in France, in a place called Lascaux, which depicts an animal with two straight horns at the center of its forehead. Because of the way the animal is drawn, the two horns can look like one, and for this reason the figure painted on the cave wall has come to be known as

'the unicorn', though some say that this 'unicorn' actually has the head of a man. In our opinion, since it is unlikely that a unicorn would stand still long enough for someone to make an accurate drawing of it, it seems most likely that this cave-painter was sketching from memory a unicorn it had seen but fleetingly, and understandably got some of the details confused.

There are thought to be further cave paintings of unicorns in Southern Africa and South America

but at present this is only hearsay. If anyone was looking for an interesting basis for an exploration of the world, they might consider searching for cave paintings of unicorns. It would certainly bring great rewards and fill out some of the details in the earliest history of unicorns.

Eastern and Western Unicorns

As there always seem to be with most creatures, there are Eastern and Western versions of the unicorn. The Eastern unicorn may not look like our traditional vision of one, but it is the oldest recorded unicorn in

history. The **Chinese Unicorn** is known as Kilin (pronounced chee-lin). It has the body of a deer, the hooves of a horse and a single short horn growing out of the middle of its forehead. Unlike the horn of the Western unicorn, that of the Kilin is made of flesh rather than bone. The hair on its back is multicolored in the five sacred Chinese colors of red, yellow, blue, white and black. The Kilin is a mixture of male and female (Ki = male; Lin = female) and it is a supremely gentle creature, careful never to tread on any living thing, lest it should cause harm or kill. The Kilin

lives for around 1000 years. In other descriptions, the Kilin is said to have the body of a deer, the head of a lion and a forwardly curved horn. Not much like a unicorn, you might say, and indeed it is probably only referred to as a Chinese unicorn because of the horn and because it brings good fortune.

The first recorded appearance of a unicorn comes in a Chinese legend. Almost five thousand years ago, a unicorn appeared to Emperor Fu Hsi and imparted to him the secret knowledge of written language. The way this happened was that the

emperor saw the markings of the Chinese characters etched on the Kilin's body. Before this, there had not been a written language, only a spoken one, but from what he saw on the unicorn's body, the Emperor Fu Hsi was able to impart the wonders of the written word to his people.

In Chinese mythology, unicorns are said to appear in order to announce important births or deaths. The birth of a famous Chinese philosopher named Confucius, who lived around 2,500 years ago, was predicted by a unicorn. When his mother was pregnant, a unicorn appeared to her as she sat under a tree. It came gently towards her, taking care not to frighten her, and laid its head in her lap. This unicorn left a small piece of jade stone in her lap with an inscription on it, telling of the great wisdom her son would possess. And it was true: Confucius was duly born and he turned out to be one of the wisest men ever to grace the earth.

The **Japanese Unicorn**, however, is an entirely different creature. It is known as Kirin and it has the body of a bull – far less delicate than the deer – and a wild, unruly mane. Unlike the Chinese unicorn, the Kirin is a creature to be feared, especially if you are a criminal. This is because the Kirin can detect guilt in people. In Japanese legend, a Kirin would be called upon during a trial; it would immediately stare at the guilty person and then pierce him or her through the heart with its horn. So you might say that the Kirin is a good creature: it points out wrong-doers and punishes them. But it does not have the gentleness and the wisdom of the Kilin. The Japanese Kirin is true and just, but it is a little too harsh in its justice.

The traditional Western unicorn has the body of a horse – the only difference being that, its hooves are cloven rather than all of one piece. The other features that make it different from a horse are the horn, its leonine tail, and its beard. The earliest mention of a unicorn in the **Western World** appears in the

writings of a Roman Historian of the 3rd century BC named Herodotus. He described a 'horned ass' living in Africa, and if you picture a 'horned ass' you pretty much get a unicorn. A century later, a Greek historian traveled to Persia where he heard of an Indian unicorn with the body of a horse. It was all white but for its head, which was red, and it had bright blue eyes and a long straight horn. These multicolored unicorns are somehow more difficult to believe in, but the fact that those who saw them are so precise and specific about their descriptions

means that we have to trust in what they saw until we see differently for ourselves.

You might expect to hear of the unicorn making an appearance in Greek mythology: there are so many other far more extraordinary beasts in Greek mythology that a unicorn would look plain ordinary. But this very ordinariness is the key, in fact, to why the unicorn does not appear in the texts of Greek mythology, because it appears instead in the texts of Greek natural history. The Ancient Greeks, along

with many others, did not doubt the real existence of the unicorn so they did not consider it to be mythological. They believed that the unicorn lived in India, a place so unknown at the time that all unusual beasts were thought to live there. Following the first identification of a unicorn by the Greek historian Ctesias, the Greek philosopher Aristotle also refers in his writings to the existence of two one-horned creatures: an Oryx (which is a horned antelope) and what he calls an 'Indian ass'.

As far as the Romans were concerned, they too put the unicorn into their books on Natural History rather than into their books on Mythology. The author of 'Natural History' named Pliny the Elder refers to an Indian ox (which was perhaps actually a rhinoceros) as well as an Indian ass, which he describes as "a very ferocious beast, similar in the rest of its body to a horse, with the head of a deer, the feet of an elephant, the tail of a boar, a deep, bellowing voice, and a single black horn, two cubits in length, standing out in the middle of its forehead." Now this may sound like an extraordinarily complicated creature, as far from our picture of an elegant unicorn as can be, but what alerts us to the possibility of this

patchwork animal actually being a unicorn is that Pliny further adds: "It cannot be taken alive", and, as we know, this is true of the unicorn.

Whether or not these fabulous beasts identified by the ancient Greeks and Romans are in fact unicorns, is in some ways irrelevant. The very fact that these ancient people also embarked on a search for a one-horned horse, as we are still today, is evidence that the magic and mystery of the unicorn was as powerfully felt then as it is now.

Famous Unicorn Sightings

The unicorn has been seen by many famous people since the world began. The very first of these was of course Adam in the Garden of Eden at the beginning of time, but since then unicorns have been sighted by Alexander the Great, who claimed to have ridden a unicorn into battle on one of his great conquests, Julius Caesar and Genghis Khan, all great and powerful leaders in their time.

Genghis Khan was one of the most fearsome warriors of his time. He conquered and ruled over Asia in the 12th century, but he still wasn't happy with what he had achieved. The story goes that, just as he was about to invade India, a unicorn appeared and knelt down before him. Genghis Khan was aghast at the sight and it humbled him. He saw the appearance of this meek and mild unicorn as a sign from heaven not to attack and consequently, he turned back his armies. As you can imagine, the people of India were eternally grateful to that unicorn. Another version of the story tells how the unicorn actually spoke, and gave Genghis Khan a piece of timely advice. It told him: 'Moderation will bring boundless pleasure'. The mighty warrior stopped to think for a moment and realized how much he already had. He decided that enough was enough – it was time to stop. And so, one of the most brutal and ruthless conquerors in the world was finally tamed by a humble unicorn.

But that was all quite a long time ago, so what about in more recent years? When was the last time

we had a positive unicorn sighting? Well, in 1663 (not so very recent, but getting there) a unicorn skeleton was supposedly found at Einhornhöhle in the Harz Mountains in Germany. Einhornhöhle translates literally as 'one horn hole' or, to put it more poetically, 'Unicorn Cave'. Although this was hailed by its discoverers as a unicorn's skeleton, it was claimed by others that the skeleton only had two legs. Furthermore, skeptics said that it wasn't genuine at all but had been painstakingly constructed out of fossilized mammoth bones. But still the discoverers

insisted that it was a unicorn skeleton and that it had two legs because souvenir-hunters had stolen the other two. The skeleton was examined by the German philosopher Leibniz, who had previously not believed in unicorns, and on seeing it, he was convinced enough to change his mind – and he was a clever man!

But someone else who didn't believe said that if the unicorn has cloven hooves – as this skeleton did – it would also have had to have a cloven skull,

and this would make the growth of a single horn impossible. But then his theory was disproven by an American professor, who succeeded in artificially fusing the horn buds of a calf together, thus creating a one-horned bull. So, the reality or otherwise of this unicorn skeleton remains a mystery to this day. Suffice to say, it has yet to be revealed as a complete hoax, as was the case with another unicorn skeleton put on display by P. T. Barnum at one of his famous circuses early in the 20th century.

Catching Unicorns

As has been said, and as anyone will tell you, unicorns are famously difficult to catch. If we could catch them, we would probably have one in a zoo somewhere, but they are extremely swift and elusive creatures. In Medieval times it was thought that, although you could never catch a unicorn by hunting it, if a beautiful virgin were to sit quietly near one, it would come over and lay its head in her lap.

There is rumored to be another method of catching unicorns, but it is unnecessarily cruel and

not at all how unicorns should be treated. The idea is that you first anger it, then run away from it towards a tree. Whilst standing in front of a tree, you wait for it to charge and when it is just about to reach you, dart out of the way so that it is impaled on the tree by its horn. This kind of entrapment renders the unicorn unconscious, deprived as it is of the power of its horn. Aside from the fact that a unicorn's dignity

should not be compromised in this way, it is also very difficult to anger unicorns, who are not easily provoked as ordinary beasts are.

The Unicorn's Horn

In *The Book of Psalms* there appears the phrase: **"My horn shall be exalted like the horn of the unicorn."** It is certainly true to say that the horn

of a unicorn is highly prized and there is very good reason for this, which you will read about hereafter.

The horn is the most precious and magical part of a unicorn. Even a sliver of unicorn horn ensures a long and healthy life to the possessor. The horn of the Indian unicorn is believed to offer protection against poison, so if poison is poured into cups made of unicorn horn, it will no longer be poisonous. For this reason, unicorn cups were used by rulers in India who feared assassination by poison and wished to avoid it.

The Secret History Of Unicorns

During medieval times, ground-up unicorn horn was a popular ingredient in many medicines, and up until the 18th century, French kings used cutlery made out of unicorn horn so that they would be protected from poison in their food. For a similar reason, the royal throne of Denmark used to be made of unicorn horn (which was actually, rather disappointingly, the tusk of another animal) to ensure the safety of the monarch. Another little-known secret is that jewelry made out of unicorn's horn can protect the wearer from evil. So a unicorn-horn necklace is an extremely precious and valuable gift. Similarly, shoes made of unicorn leather guarantee healthy feet and belts made of unicorn leather ward off sickness of the stomach.

Not surprisingly, the unicorn's horn is worth more than its weight in gold. It is said that Queen Elizabeth I owned a complete unicorn horn and it was valued at £10,000, which at the time was enough money to buy a large castle. Various other kings and popes are said to have owned unicorn horns, but they couldn't always be sure that they were getting the real thing. The horn of a narwhal – which looks very similar to that of the unicorn – was often used by crooked dealers in place of genuine unicorn horn and in this way, many rich fools were deceived. Other popular substitutes were elephant's tusk and stag's horn. As you can imagine, these dishonest traders in unicorn horn, made a fortune fooling the gullible rich who thought that they were buying the promise of good health, or even immortality.

Distinguishing True Unicorn Horn from False Ones

So, how can you tell a real unicorn horn from fake? It's a tricky one, but fortunately, over the years, a number of tests have been devised to detect, whether or not, a piece of horn genuinely belongs to a unicorn or not. (Most of these can safely be tried at home but you might like to seek advice before you attempt to carry out some of the more hazardous tests!)

• Find a spider and draw a ring around it on the floor with the horn. If the horn is genuine, the spider will not be able to cross the ring you have drawn on the floor.

• Put some scorpions in a pot with the horn and cover it with a lid. Leave it for three to four hours and if, when you lift the lid the scorpions are dead, the horn is genuine.

• Place the horn in cold water. If the water 'boils' but remains cold, the horn is genuine.

• Feed arsenic to a pigeon and then immediately give it some ground-up horn. If the pigeon lives, the horn is genuine.

Unicorn Hair

Whilst the unicorn's horn is undoubtedly its most precious feature, its hair also has magical properties. Unicorn hair has been used in the art of wand-making for many centuries. Its silvery moon-like aura lends the wand a magical luminescence and, because of the purity of the unicorn's spirit, unicorn hair can only make wands which are to be used for good ends. So, you would never find a unicorn-hair wand in the hands of an evil magician because it simply wouldn't work.

Unicorns in Art

Unicorns were very popular in medieval times and many of our favorite images of unicorns come from tapestries woven during those times. There is a particularly famous tapestry called 'The Hunt of the Unicorn', which was woven in Belgium in the 16th century and today hangs in a museum in New York. There are actually seven tapestries, each depicting a scene from a hunt at which well-dressed noblemen, accompanied by huntsmen and hounds, pursue

a unicorn through a landscape of elegant houses and well-tended gardens. They tame the unicorn with the help of a maiden, who entraps it with her beauty. In the next scene, the noblemen appear to kill the unicorn, and bring it back in triumph to their castle, but in the last scene, named "The Unicorn in Captivity", the unicorn is shown alive again. This final tapestry depicts the unicorn chained to a tree and surrounded by a fence in a field of flowers. The tree is a pomegranate tree, and although there are red stains on the unicorn's white coat, some say that they are the stains of pomegranate juice rather than blood. Pomegranates were at the time a positive symbol, suggesting the joy of fertility, and this final scene is thought by some to depict a happy unicorn, content to be tamed by its hunters. However, the true meaning of this last tapestry, in which the unicorn has mysteriously been brought back from the dead, is unclear.

There is another set of six tapestries now kept in France called *Dame á La Licorne* (Lady with the unicorn). This was woven in the Netherlands at about the same time as The Hunt of the Unicorn, and it depicts the five senses – sight, smell, taste, touch and hearing – which, in medieval times were seen as the gateways to temptation. In this work of art, the unicorn seems to be linked to worldly temptations. The final tapestry is called "To my only desire" ("A mon seul désir").

During medieval times, the unicorn was generally used as a symbol of both spiritual love and romantic love. Pictures of unicorns laying their heads in the laps of young women were particularly popular at the time. To some, the unicorn represented Christ and the young woman the Virgin Mary, but to others it was more to do with the love between a man and a woman. In the literature of medieval France, the hero of a story often compared the strength of his love for his beloved with that shown by the unicorn for the young woman. So there were many different ways of viewing the unicorn in medieval times, but it always stood for love, gentleness and dignity.

An Italian explorer called Marco Polo confidently asserts that the unicorn is not at all as everyone imagines it: a beautiful, shining, magical beast, but ugly and dirty. He wrote:

"They are scarcely smaller than elephants. They have the hair of a buffalo and feet like an elephant's. They have a single large black horn in the middle of the forehead... They have a head like a wild boar's... They spend their time by preference wallowing in mud and slime. They are very ugly brutes to look at. They are not at all such as we describe them when we relate that they let themselves be captured by virgins, but clean contrary to our notions."

Unfortunately for Marco Polo (but luckily for us unicorn lovers) what he had actually seen was a rhinoceros, not a unicorn at all. Lucky also for all those young women in the medieval paintings, as it wouldn't be very pleasant to have a rhinoceros laying its head in your lap.

Unicorns and Christianity

Due to its single horn, the unicorn has often been used as a spiritual symbol. Saint Ambrose, the Bishop of Milan in the 4th century, compared the unicorn's horn to Christ because he was the single and unique son of God. Another Christian saint, Saint Augustine, said that the unicorn's horn was like the single faith of the Church. These sorts of comparisons have helped to strengthen the idea of the unicorn's goodness and purity.

The unicorn can even be found hiding in the pages of the Bible, and there is an intriguing story behind its shadowy appearance there. There is a

creature in the Bible called in Hebrew a re'em, which is often used as a symbol of great strength. Actually, it is now thought to refer to a buffalo native to Lebanon, known as a 'rimu', a powerful creature with two horns, but at the time of the King James translation of the Bible in 17th century England, 're'em' was translated as 'unicorn', and so we have phrases in the Bible such as 'His strength is as the strength of the unicorn'. One reason behind this is that in ancient drawings of the rimu, its two horns appear to be one (as in the cave paintings described earlier). So the rimu was thought to be a sort of unicorn. What is amazing about this is how the unicorn has calmly and quietly walked into the pages of this most sacred book, to stand as a symbol of pure strength, almost without anyone noticing it.

The Unicorn in the Sky

If you have never seen a unicorn and fear that you never will, do not despair, for there is one place that you can be sure of seeing one and that is in the night sky. If you look up into the heavens at night, you might see the constellation called **Monoceros**, which is Greek for 'single horn' (there's one new name for you!). For obvious reasons, this is also known as the unicorn constellation: it is made up of 146 stars and the Milky Way runs right through the middle of it. Take a look.

Unicorns – real or mythical creatures

In ancient days, the existence of unicorns was not doubted. In Medieval times, for example, it was firmly believed that they existed, the only problem was trying to see one or catch one. Gradually, however, as time passed and science developed, people became more suspicious of things, they could not prove. Since

no one could prove the existence of the unicorn, it gradually turned into a 'mythical' creature. In the ninth century, one writer complained:

'It is universally held that the unicorn is a supernatural being and of auspicious omen; so say the odes, the annals, the biographies of worthies, and other texts whose authority is unimpeachable. Even village women and children know the unicorn is a lucky sign. But this animal does not figure

among the barnyard animals, it is not always easy to come across, it does not lend itself to zoological classification, nor is it like the horse or bull, the wolf or deer. In such circumstances, we may be face to face with a unicorn and not know for sure that we are. We know a certain animal with a mane is a horse and that a certain animal with horns is a bull. We do not know what the unicorn looks like'.

Thoughts such as these that banish magic and do not allow for the possible existence of what cannot be seen, have gradually rid the unicorn of its status as a real creature. What had previously been sightings of unicorns are now presumed to be sightings of rhinos, goats or antelopes. Now that there are precise systems in place for recording and classifying all types of creatures, unicorns will probably never be

considered real again, but this does not matter one bit to the unicorns. In fact, it is probably to their advantage. And they will continue to exist, whether or not they are classified and recorded. It now seems that the men of medieval times who believed in unicorns were more intelligent than us, because they knew that there were different kinds of realities and that you didn't have to be able to see or touch something for it to exist.

Possible Impostors

So, if unicorns had never lived and breathed on this earth (or, rather, if they haven't been careless enough

to leave their bones lying around after they have gone) what *is* it that all these people who claim to have seen them have really seen? Well, here are some possible suggestions:

The Elasmotherium

It has sometimes been suggested that what passes for the unicorn is really an extinct animal sometimes called the "Giant Unicorn" but known to scientists as Elasmotherium. The Elasmotherium is a huge creature, similar to the wooly rhinoceros, which is native to the Steppes of Eastern Europe. In its day, it looked something like a horse, but it had a large single

horn in its forehead. It is thought to have lived during the Ice Age, but it seems to have become extinct about the same time as the rest of the vast beasts that inhabited the glacial age. However, there is a chance that it may have survived beyond these times, which would account for some of the more recent sightings. Evidence that Elasmotherium did survive beyond the end of the Ice Age appears in the legends of the Evenk people of Russia, as a huge black bull with a single horn in the middle of its forehead.

Furthermore, the medieval traveler Ibn Fadlan, who is usually considered a trustworthy source had left behind an account of what appears to be Elasmotherium:

> *"There is nearby a wide steppe, and there dwells, it is told, an animal smaller than a camel, but taller than a bull. Its head is the head of a ram, and its tail is a bull's tail. Its body is that of a mule and its hooves are like those of a bull. In the middle of its head it has a horn, thick and round, and as the*

horn goes higher, it narrows (to an end), until it is like a spearhead. Some of these horns grow to three or five ells, depending on the size of the animal. It thrives on the leaves of trees, which are excellent greenery. Whenever it sees a rider, it approaches and if the rider has a fast horse, the horse tries to escape by running fast, and if the beast overtakes them, it picks the rider out of the saddle with its horn, and tosses him in the air, and meets him with the point of the horn, and continues doing so until the rider dies.

But it will not harm or hurt the horse in any way or manner.

"The locals seek it in the steppe and in the forest until they can kill it. It is done so: they climb the tall trees between which the animal passes. It requires several bowmen with poisoned arrows; and when the beast is in between them, they shoot and wound it unto its death. And indeed I have seen three big bowls shaped like Yemen seashells, that the king has, and he told me that they are made out of that animal's horn."

However, the vicious behavior of this creature and its dark, stocky appearance make it a very unconvincing substitute for a unicorn. There is none of the magic or the majesty in this beast that we associate with the unicorn.

A mutant goat

It has elsewhere been suggested that the unicorn is really a mutant goat. Well, we can tell already that we are not going to be convinced by this unflattering comparison. The connection that has been made between a single-horned goat and a unicorn is due

to a vision of Daniel recorded in the Bible (*Book of Daniel* 8:5)

> *And as I was considering, behold, a he-goat came from the west over the face of the whole earth, and touched not the ground: and the goat had a notable horn between his eyes.*

There is evidence of a rare deformity occurring in the domestic goat whereby the two horns are joined together; such an animal could be another possible inspiration for the legend. There have been incidents in the past of unscrupulous people determined to make money out of the unicorn

producing fake unicorns by remodeling the "horn buttons" of goat kids in such a way that their two horns became one. But these barbaric practices have nothing to do with the unicorn, whose beautiful and perfectly proportioned body could never be the result of deformities in nature.

The Narwhal

The Narwhal, an Arctic cetacean, has spiral tusks like the unicorn and this shared feature has led rogue traders in the past to pass Narwhal tusk off as unicorn horn. Precious objects ornamented with supposed

unicorn horn can be found in museums in places like Vienna, but they are now recognized to be made of Narwhal tusk. These tusks were probably brought to Europe by the Vikings, or other sea-farers from the Northern parts, and sold as genuine unicorn horns to the gullible natives when they invaded.

The Oryx

The Oryx is an antelope with two long, thin horns emerging from its forehead. Some have suggested that if you view the Oryx from the side and at a distance, it can look something like a horse with a single horn. However, an important difference is that the 'horn' of the Oryx leans backwards rather than

forwards as the unicorn's does. It is certainly possible that some people who claim to have seen a unicorn have actually only seen an Oryx, but this does not detract from the reality of unicorns. In literature, the Oryx and the unicorn appear as separate creatures existing at the same time, so while the Oryx may in the past have been mistaken for a unicorn, this does not mean that the unicorn is in fact an Oryx.

Besides, these rather dull explanations take all the magic away from unicorns, which are not after all meant to be classified like ordinary creatures. One thing is certain is that none of these supposed substitutions will ever satisfy the genuine lover of unicorns, who will know deep down that they are not really true. The reason is that a unicorn is entirely unique and comparing it to other animals simply does not work.

If the unicorn is to be denied a proper place in natural history, it at least lives on in literature, which really is its true and natural home. Unicorns are perfectly alive in a number of stories, and the fact that they are stories does not make the unicorns any less real.

Heraldry

But before we get into telling stories about unicorns, it is worth mentioning that there is another place – apart from in literature – where unicorns live on, untarnished and untroubled, and that is in heraldry. Coats of arms have, since medieval times, used mythical creatures symbolically to represent

people and places, qualities and attributes. We call these creatures 'mythical' in the sense that they are hybrids of other animals rather than complete animals themselves. So the 'lion' in the Prince of Wales' coat of arms, for example, is actually a beast with the head of a lion, the body of a leopard, and the feet of a bear.

In heraldry, a unicorn is depicted as a horse with a goat's cloven hooves and beard, a lion's tail, and a slender, spiral horn on its forehead. The unicorn's most important place in heraldry is in the royal arms of Scotland and, because Scotland is part of the United Kingdom, it appears in the arms of the United Kingdom as well. There is no definite answer as to what the unicorn represents in heraldry, but

what is interesting is, that it is usually collared and chained. If the unicorn is seen as a representation of raw animal passions, the chained unicorn indicates restraint in that area. The unicorn also appears on the Coat of Arms of the Prince of Wales (Prince Charles), where it represents Scotland and is found chained to the red dragon which represents Wales.

Unicorns in Literature

Folk Tales

There are many folk tales from Britain about the magic of unicorns, even one where King Arthur, as a newly crowned king, meets a unicorn on a remote Scottish island. This unicorn has nurtured a baby boy who was abandoned there and it has turned into

The Secret History Of Unicorns

a giant. King Arthur sees a halo around the unicorn's head and feels completely at peace in his presence, and although he knows that this is a remarkable beast and that he would achieve fame if he brought it home with him, he also knows instantly that the unicorn is sacred and precious and should never be hunted, and that is what he teaches his people when he returns home.

The image of the Lion and the Unicorn holding up the crown which appears on the Royal Coat of Arms of the United Kingdom has given birth to a host of stories about the struggle for supremacy between these two noble creatures.

There is in England an old song which goes:

The Lion and the Unicorn were fighting for the crown:
The Lion beat the Unicorn all around the town.

Some gave them white bread, some gave them brown:
Some gave them plum-cake and drummed them out of town.

Here is a **folk-tale** about the lion and the unicorn, which celebrates the joys of friendship and the benefits of helping each other.

'The Lion and the Unicorn'

The Lion and the Unicorn were forever fighting over the crown:

"It's mine."

"No, it's mine."

"No, mine."

"I touched it first."

"No, I did."

And so it went on, hour after hour, day after day, year after year, as they scrapped and squabbled over the crown, until one day they had finally had enough. It was a bright sunny day, and suddenly they didn't feel like fighting any more.

The Lion said to the Unicorn: "Look here, I'm worn out. My paws are torn, my mane is a mess of tangles and my tail is full of dust. Let's stop." The Unicorn replied: "Thank goodness! I'm tired out too: my spiral horn is chipped all over and my silver hooves need a new coat of paint they're so scratched up." They sat down in the shade of a tree and they both sighed with relief, glad to be able to enjoy the sunny day and each other's

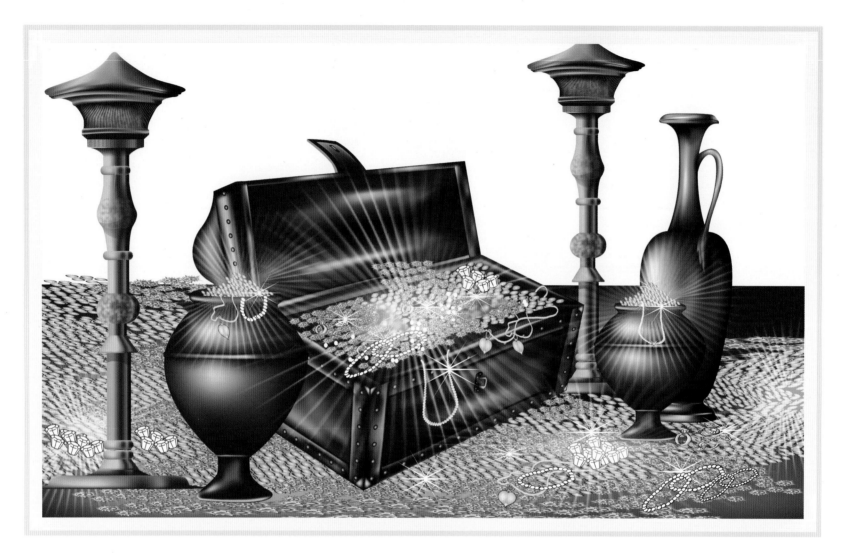

company at last. The Unicorn found a precious comb made of carved bone and gently began to comb the tangles out of the Lion's bedraggled mane. Then, he brushed all the dust out of the Lion's tail and washed it through with some clear spring water. Feeling much better, the Lion went in search of a pot of gold paint and a pot of silver paint. He came back with the paint and the brush and said to the Unicorn

"Hold still while I repaint you, I don't want it to smudge."

And with great care, the Lion repainted the spiral horn gold and the chipped hooves silver, until the Unicorn gleamed in the sunlight.

"I'm hungry," said the Lion, "let's go and have some tea." So they strolled off to a tea-shop, arm in arm, in the evening sun and forgot all about fighting each other.

The same lion and unicorn also appear in **'Through the Looking Glass'** by Lewis Carroll. In this episode of Alice's adventures, the whole question of whether unicorns are real or mythical is turned completely on its head. *Alice is with the White King when they hear of a fight between the lion and the unicorn who hold up the King's crown. The King thinks it ridiculous, since it is his crown anyway, and neither of them will get it even if they do win the fight, but they rush to watch the fight all the same and when it is over the Unicorn – who is rather*

an arrogant creature – saunters carelessly by, boasting of his success:

He was going on, when his eye happened to fall upon Alice: he turned round instantly, and stood for some time looking at her with an air of the deepest disgust.

"What is this?" he said at last.

"This is a child!" Haigha replied eagerly, coming in front of Alice to introduce her. "We only found it today. It's as large as life, and twice as natural!"

"I always thought they were fabulous monsters!" said the Unicorn. "Is it alive?"

"It can talk," said Haigha solemnly.

The Unicorn looked dreamily at Alice, and said "Talk, child."

Alice could not help her lips curling up into a smile as she began:

"Do you know, I always thought Unicorns were fabulous monsters, too? I never saw one alive before!"

"Well, now that we have seen each other,' said the Unicorn, "if you'll believe in me, I'll believe in you. Is that a bargain?"

`Yes, if you like,' said Alice.

This Scottish folk-tale illustrates the great, unspoken power of the unicorn and its protective instincts. It also warns us of the danger of not believing in magical creatures.

'The Fair Maid and the Snow-White Unicorn'

A long time ago, when people still believed in magic, there lived in a crumbling castle a fair maid with eyes as black as berries and skin as white as apple blossom. Her family had

once been rich and powerful and the castle in all its splendor had been the envy of all the Lords and Ladies in the land. They had once had fine clothes and jewels, servants and soldiers, but now the Fair Maid with eyes as black as berries and skin as white as apple blossom was all that was left of that once glorious family. She wore rags in place of her velvet gowns and she went barefoot, even in winter.

Since she could no longer afford soldiers and servants to look after her, she had been given a unicorn as her guardian. He was a beautiful creature, as white as the snow; he had a horn growing from the middle of his velvety forehead and blue eyes, as blue as the sea. The Fair Maid and her unicorn went everywhere together and soon people began to talk of this strange sight – the barefoot girl and her blue-eyed unicorn

roaming around the hills together. Some young men, sons of the greatest Lords and Ladies in the land, decided one day that they would hunt this unicorn and kill it and then they would woo the Fair Maid.

They galloped over the hills on their fine horses until they came in sight of the ruined castle and there, in the overgrown garden, they saw the maid and her unicorn and they were stunned by the beauty of both. Each young man prepared in turn to draw his bow and shoot a deadly arrow into the unicorn's side, but each time they pulled back the arrow, the unicorn shook its head and they were paralyzed, completely unable to move or speak. The men were too ashamed to tell

each other what had happened, so they all pretended that they didn't want to woo the maid anyway. She was ugly and no more than a beggar, and they all rode home. None of them ever told anyone what had happened to them when the unicorn shook its head. Instead, they told everyone that the maid was ugly and no more than a beggar, and that the unicorn was nothing special either.

Now the maid had never left her falling-down castle, but one spring morning, she had a thirst for adventure and she wandered over hills and vales with her unicorn until they reached a stone farmhouse surrounded by fields of thick heather. There was a sighing on the air and the Fair Maid asked the unicorn:

"What is that sound?"

"It is only the wind blowing through the heather," he replied.

"No it is more than that," said the maid, "It is the sound of sorrow – there are some unhappy people here."

No sooner did she speak than a little man popped out of the heather.

"You are right," he said. "We are the last of the Little People and we have just been thrown out of the farmhouse that we used to make our home. We have nowhere to go and no one will feed us."

The Fair Maid thought about her empty, draughty tumble-down castle and said immediately,

"Well you must come home with me. You can live in the corner by the fire and I will feed you."

So, the Little People returned gratefully to the castle and were soon, quite at home. Over the next days and weeks, they set to work with their tiny hammers, repairing the castle until it was quite restored to its original splendor, with tapestries on the walls and the finest furnishings in the land. The Fair Maid was delighted with her new home and she asked the oldest and wisest of the Little People,

"How can I repay you for what you have done?"

"All I ask is that you follow a small piece of advice: you must find a husband to take care of you and be master of this castle."

So word was sent out that the Fair Maid was looking for a husband and would accept suitors on the first day of May.

The first day of May came and suitors came from far and wide – princes from the North, East, South and West. The Fair Maid thought each was dazzlingly handsome, courageous and strong – for she had never seen a man before – but before she would consent to marry any of them she asked one simple question:

"Will there be a place for the Little People in our castle?"

Each handsome prince answered just the same:

"The Little People? Why, they haven't been around for years, and a good thing too – they were nothing but trouble."

So the maid could not consent to marry any of the dashing princes who had traveled so far and each was sent back to where he came from.

When the last prince had left, and the door of the castle had shut behind him, the Fair Maid sat down by the fire, turned to the unicorn and sighed:

"Dear, sweet, wise unicorn. If I had asked you if there would be place for the Little People in our castle, what would you have said?"

"Always," the unicorn answered.

The Fair Maid thought for a moment about how the unicorn had always been by her side, protecting her, comforting her, a constant companion, and she said:

"Then I shall marry you."

And at that moment the unicorn disappeared and in his place stood a handsome prince who was not only handsome, but brave, kind and gentle too! So, she married her unicorn prince and they lived in the beautiful castle with the Little People happily ever after.

Another folk-tale from England illustrates the unicorn's generous nature, ever willing to help others.

'The Unicorn who walks alone'

The unicorn, as we know, is by nature a solitary creature, but whenever he is needed, he does not hesitate to respond. *Once, long ago, in a deep forest, there lived all manner of creatures – large and small, fierce and gentle – and the unicorn lived with them, but he kept aloof. There was a terrible drought at this time and all the trees had lost their greenery, the grass was burnt crisp in the relentless sun and the ground was hard and dry. But the pool where the animals drank every evening remained full to the brim and so they were all able to quench their thirst.*

Another folk tale from England illustrates the unicorn's generous nature, ever willing to help others.

But one day, when no one else was at the pool, a malevolent snake slithered to the pool and spat his venom all over the surface, then he slithered off, pleased with his malicious work. That evening, the animals gathered as usual to drink their fill at the pool, but as soon as they reached the water's edge, they could smell the poison and they knew that if they drank the water, they would die. The animals didn't know what to do: some wept, some howled, some roared with anger. 'Was there no one who could help them?' they cried. Gradually more animals gathered, even those who would never normally drink together at the pool and who would usually fight each other, but no one fought. They all just stood there and wondered what to do.

The unicorn, who was wandering alone elsewhere in the forest, heard their cries and knew instantly what was wrong by the sound. He galloped to where they all stood around the poisoned pool and without a sound, knelt down and dipped his horn in the pool. He lowered his head until the whole horn was in the water and then drew it out again and they could see that all the poison was gone and the water was as pure as could be. Without any pushing or quarreling, the animals lowered their heads in turn and drank deep from the pure, clear water, but when they looked around to thank the unicorn, for what he had done, the unicorn had gone.

The Secret History Of Unicorns

There is a story by the American humorist James Thurber called 'The Unicorn in the Garden' which warns us of the dangers of not believing in magic and it goes something like this.

'The Unicorn in the Garden'

One morning, a man woke up feeling very happy and looked out into his garden. There he saw, to his surprise, a unicorn standing amongst the flower beds, quietly munching on some sweet roses. He was so surprised and delighted that he went and woke up his wife — who he didn't like very much — to tell her that there was a unicorn in the garden. His wife — who didn't like him very much either — was seriously displeased. She told him:

There is a story by the American humorist James Thurber called 'The Unicorn in the Garden' which warns us of the dangers of not believing in magic.

"Don't be ridiculous: unicorns don't exist, they are mythical creatures. How can there be one in the garden?"

"Well there is," he told her, "it has a golden horn in the middle of its head and it is eating the flowers."

But his wife just ignored him, so he went out into the garden, where the unicorn was still munching quietly at the flowers. He picked a white lily and handed it to the unicorn and the unicorn ate it right out of his hands. The man was

astonished and he went back inside to tell his wife that the unicorn had eaten a lily out of his hand. But his wife still wouldn't believe him; she just told him he was mad and should be sent to the mad-house. In fact, as soon as he had gone, she telephoned a psychiatrist and the police and told them both:

"My husband told me there was a unicorn in our garden with a golden horn and it ate a lily out of his hand. Bring a straight-jacket when you come."

The psychiatrist turned up at the house and the police turned up at the house, and they had brought a straight-jacket

The Secret History Of Unicorns

as she had instructed. *They asked the wife to repeat what she had told them and she did, so they took hold of her and put her in a straight-jacket.*

"You must be mad," they told her, "unicorns don't exist."

When the man came back into the house, they asked him if he had told his wife that there was a

unicorn in the garden with a golden horn and that it ate a lily out of his hand.

"Don't be ridiculous," he said, "unicorns don't exist, they are mythical creatures. How could there be one in the garden?"

And so the grumpy wife was carted off to the mad-house.

Pegasus

The mythical flying horse known as Pegasus is not strictly a unicorn, but he is just as magical and could easily be counted as a distant cousin. Indeed, some consider him to be a form of unicorn, since the unicorn does not appear elsewhere in Greek mythology, and so we will tell his tale here, lest he should be forgotten by future generations.

Pegasus, the winged white stallion, was the child of Poseidon, God of the sea, and the beautiful virgin,

Medusa, a handmaiden in the temple of Athena. Poseidon was so taken with Medusa's beauty that he seduced her within the walls of Athena's temple. Athena was furious about this violation of her temple, but she could not punish Poseidon as he was a god, so she turned her fury on Medusa. She transformed her into a hideous monster with serpents for hair and a face so vile that the sight of it turned any who looked

on it to stone. Medusa was banished to the island of the Gorgons so that she would not turn the world to stone.

The Greek Hero Perseus, was given the difficult task of beheading Medusa as a test of his strength and ingenuity. The difficult part was cutting her head off without looking at her; as, if he did, he would be

turned to stone. But he solved this problem by reflecting on her image in his shield, and so avoided looking directly at her, and with one stroke of his sword, he cut off Medusa's head.

It was out of Medusa's severed neck that Pegasus was born. Perhaps surprisingly, since he came from such hideous beginnings, Pegasus was a beautiful white horse with wings. Instead of being turned to stone, those who gazed at Pegasus simply gasped

in awe and wonder. When Athena found out about Pegasus, she gave the Greek Hero, Bellerophon, a golden bridle to tame him. While Pegasus was drinking from a stream, Bellerophon approached

him from behind and threw the bridle over his head. Bellerophon jumped on Pegasus' back and they became as one – inseparable friends. Pegasus and Bellerophon galloped over land and sea faster than the wind. While riding Pegasus, Bellerophon knew

no bounds, and one day he attempted to fly Pegasus up to Mount Olympus to join the gods. Zeus punished Bellerophon's insolence by having a horsefly sting Pegasus, causing Bellerophon to fall from his steed and come crashing back to Earth.

Now that he was alone, Pegasus flew to Mount Olympus himself where he was welcomed by the gods and where Zeus made him the carrier of his thunderbolts. As a special honor to mark his tireless service to the gods, Zeus set the constellation off the winged horse in the Earth's night sky. And there it lies - the constellation 'Pegasus' - between Pisces and Andromeda.

If you would like to read more fiction in which unicorns appear, you could check out some of the following books:

- Madeline L'Engle's *A Swiftly Tilting Planet and Many Waters*

- C. S. Lewis's *The Last Battle*

- Kathleen Duey's *Moonsilver, The Journey Home and Mountains of the Moon*

- Geraldine McCaughrean's *Unicorns! Unicorns!*

- Michael Morpurgo's *I Believe in Unicorns*

- Patricia Finney's *Unicorn Blood*